SUSAN LYNN SOLOMON

'TWAS THE SEASON

Secret Santa

An Emlyn Goode Mystery

ALL RIGHTS RESERVED

Publisher's Note:

This is a work of fiction. All names, characters, places, and events are the work of the author's imagination.

Any resemblance to real persons, places, or events is coincidental.

Solstice Publishing -
www.solsticepublishing.com

'Twas the Season

An Emlyn Goode Mystery

Susan Lynn Solmon

To a dear friend

Renee Balassone Wade,

with thanks for her support and encouragement

Chapter One
Was the Night before Christmas

I don't know how I get involved these things. I truly don't. It isn't as if I wake in the morning and think, *What shall I do today? Oh, I know—I'll go out and search for a murderer, then get in Roger's way while he tries to solve the case.* It's just that when someone is murdered in my small city, someone I know, I get angry (neither a safe nor even sane state for someone with my heritage), and can't stop myself until I figure out the *who* and *why*. Yes, I know the police will be hunting for the killer. But they move so slowly and, I have to admit, patience is not one of my strong suits. This time it happened on December 24, the start of the season of peace and joy… until it wasn't.

"Get a move on, Emlyn. We're, gonna be late!" Roger called from the bottom of the stairs.

In the bathroom on the second floor, I called back, "I'm getting ready as fast as I can."

I lived in a two story cottage on River Road, bet-ween the City of Niagara Falls and the Town of North Tonawanda.

Detective Roger Frey owned the house next door, though for months he'd all but lived in my house… and, not because there was construction going on at his.

Holding back my long red hair, I leaned over the sink, and flicked black mascara on my lashes. Then I blinked, and stood back, muttering, "Damn!"

Elvira, the albino pain in my derriere, looked up from where she had parked herself at my feet. She mewed, as if to say, *Watch it! You're making a mess.*

"Instead of sitting here, cat," I said, "why don't you keep him busy until I'm done?"

She tilted her head, and looked at me with her impossibly pink eyes. Again she mewed. This time it was as if she said, *Yeah. Right.*

With a groan, I fixed the smudge near the edge of my upper eyelid.

"Let's go!" Roger called.

I heard the hall closet door open.

Men, I thought as, followed by my cat, I started down the stairs. *They have no idea what it takes for a woman to look presentable.*

At the open front door, his head turned to look out-side, Roger held my coat. "What's taking so long?"

I stopped at the hall mirror to check my makeup one last time. Red headed women are told not to wear red. I paid as much attention to this rule as I did to most others. My red wool dress with a cowl collar fell just above my knees, and flattered my five-foot-seven frame. My gold chandelier earrings studded with jade showed off my neck.

"You want me to look good for your friends, don't you?" I said.

"Emlyn!"

"Relax, Roger. We'll be on time for the party."

Elvira smacked his leg with her paw, then shot him a look that said, *What's wrong with you? Tell her she looks nice.*

Of course, I had no idea if that's what the cat meant, but it certainly was what *I* thought.

Roger got the message. Standing at the front door, he wrapped me in my coat and then in his arms. "You look… Wow!"

The moment was lost when he smacked my rear, and said, "Okay, let's get rolling."

As I said, men!

"Aren't you going to warm up the car?" I asked.

He held the glass storm door for me. "I did that ten minutes ago."

I clutched his arm as we walked down the path to my driveway. I had to hold on, because freezing rain the night before had left the path icy. Though my guy had gone out early that morning to spread salt, the leather soles of my dressy boots still made walking tenuous.

When we were at last in his Trailblazer, he backed out of my driveway. As we turned onto Williams Road, I asked, "Who'd you draw for the Secret Santa?"

He smiled, but didn't answer.

With my fingers, I traced his cheekbone, then worked the design up to his graying sideburn, a reminder of the design I'd drawn on his thigh last night. "Roger, who'd you get?"

"You know we're not supposed to tell." His smile grew until it showed the gap between his front teeth.

I blew in his ear. "Please? You can tell *me*."

He gently pushed my face away, "Stop it. You'll get us into an accident."

I sat back, grinning. "Tell me, and I'll behave."

"You'll never behave. It's one of the things I like most about you."

"That's not an answer."

"You're such a snoop." He laughed. "Okay, okay. Stay in your seat. I got Collins."

I smiled. A woman didn't need a gun to get infor-mation from a guy—especially if that guy was in love with her. "So, what are you giving him?"

"A gold pocket watch."

My eyes went wide. "A what? Harry said no one was supposed to spend more than fifteen dollars on a gift."

Staring straight ahead, Roger said, "I didn't spend anything. The watch was my grandfather's."

Roger's grandfather had been a conductor on the New York Central Railroad.

"B-but t-that watch is your family's heirloom."

"I talked to my mother and brother about this. They know why I have to do it. Fact is, they agreed."

My eyes narrowed, I stared at him.

His expression serious, he said, "Someone saves the life of the woman I intend to marry… a man remembers that."

I gulped, recalling the incident he spoke of. A former rock star had been murdered, then her killer had come after me. I would have been the man's next victim if Officer Collins hadn't burst in.

Roger shifted his head slightly. With the kind of look that sometimes melted my heart, he continued, "So, Christmas here, you wanna finally agree to be my wife?"

Again I gulped. Sure, I loved this man. But marriage? The idea of taking that step frightened me more than a killer with a pistol standing in my living room. I'd walked along that track once and been run down by a train named Kevin Reinhart, a man who had trouble keeping his fly zipped. Yes, my fear was unreasonable. Roger was nothing like my ex. Still, I had built a nice life as a single woman, an author, who could come and go as I pleased. Marriage would end all that… Wouldn't it?

"We can talk about that later," I said. "We're almost at the Echo Club."

I hoped a few drinks at his precinct's Christmas party would put the idea of marriage out of his mind. At least, for a while.

Chapter Two
All Through the House

We turned off the Niagara Scenic Parkway at the traffic circle, the last exit before the road led to lots where people parked to watch the Niagara River tumble over the falls. A right on Buffalo Avenue, then left on Portage Road brought us to one of my city's historic buildings. The Echo Club, a five-floor edifice built in 1885 as a twenty-four-room mansion by the philanthropist, Thomas V. Welch, had a storied—and haunted—past. When Welch died (his great wealth couldn't save him from the ravages of typhoid fever), his mansion was sold to Alexander Zaleski, a Polish immigrant. Zaleski used the building as a credit union and a club for the Polish community. Sometime around 1930, he died of a heart attack in the basement but, according to legend, he never left. After his death, or perhaps, while he still lived, a bar in the secret basement served the community (literally) during prohibition. This site of a former prohibition bar had been selected by the officers in Roger's precinct as the site of their annual Christmas celebration.

"We're late," Roger complained, as he crawled up the block in search of a place to park.

I considered tossing out a spell that would drive someone from their home in a mad dash to move their car (a direct descendant of Sarah Goode, a supposed witch of Salem fame, my ancient relative's supposed… uh, 'skills' ran in my genes). When I glanced at Roger, I thought better of hexing our way into a parking spot. Having learned of my heritage less than two years earlier I was new to this witch-thing, so it was quite possible the homeowner would rush to his car, because I had inadvertently set his house on fire.

I guess the god and goddess decided to reward me for my rare show of restraint. A moment later, a spot opened up across the street. Making a quick U-turn, Roger slid his Trailblazer into it.

I glanced at my watch as I stepped from the car. "Just past eight-thirty," I said. "We're not terribly late."

The response I received was a terse, "Not *terribly*." But, then he smiled and reached for my arm. In the spirit of the season, I'd been forgiven.

He guided me across the street, through an iron gate, and along a gently winding path. In front of us, guarded by evergreen trees, Tom Welch's former mansion rose from gray stone foundations. The gray stone formed the walls of the lower floors, and the pillars that supported the overhanging upper floors. Above the stonework were windowed white stucco walls, and a red shingled A-frame roof over each wing of the house.

On the second floor, we entered a room with a long, brown-veneer bar. An antique copper spittoon, reminiscent of the bar's past, was placed where it curved. Groups of men and women, glasses in their hands, were talking near the bar. Others were seated at square tables. After ordering drinks (chardonnay for me, scotch for him), Roger led me to one of the tables, where he rested his hand on the shoulder of a man with a long, horsey face.

"How goes it, Scott," he said.

The man turned from the woman with whom he had been speaking. "Doing good, Roger. Got that Street case wrapped just a few weeks after it happened."

"I read your report. Great work." Roger pulled out a chair for me to sit. Taking a seat next to me, he continued,

"How'd you come to it being Derek Street who heisted that jewelry from Firth's?"

I blinked. I knew Derek Street. Not well, but I'd met him. He and my ex had hung out together, and had been partners in what Kevin called business deals.

Scott raised his tumbler. "Got a line on him from Ruben's Buy and Sell over on Pine Avenue. The moron sold Ruben's a pair of diamond studs, then went to the casino with the money. Took a lotta legwork. Still haven't figured how he knew Firth's would be shut for construction work that day. Best bet, someone was in on the heist with him—too big a deal for a smalltime thief like Street to pull off on his own. Don't know who, but a bit more legwork will get me the answers."

"Yeah, legwork." Roger shifted his eyes to me, and smiled. He constantly told me police legwork, not getting ideas after sniffing incense, was how crimes were solved. "That's the reason you need to stay outta my cases and let me do my job," he would say.

I smacked his arm. "You didn't say that when I showed you who killed Heather Munroe, and—"

He shook his head. "You were lucky a couple of times, but luck runs out and can get you hurt."

Scott laughed. Raising his glass to me, he said, "You must be Emlyn. Never heard of anyone else who could put Roger in his place."

I bowed my head.

"Emlyn Goode?" Wide eyed, the woman next to Scott stared are me. "I've read your books. Loved them." She put out her hand. "I'm Ginny Potter, Scott's wife. I've always wanted to write. How did you get started?"

Ginny Potter was a petite blonde, and appeared to be just past forty, the same age as I. She had a pug nose and thin lips. For the next little while, she and I spoke about writing, while our guys told each other war stories about the cases they'd worked.

Soon, another couple pulled over chairs, and joined our conversation. I knew these people. Friends of Roger's, we had gone out to dinner with them a number of times. Alice Cummings, a raven haired former Peach Festival queen, worked in Niagara County's IT department. Her husband, Dan, had alert blue-eyes and a jaw as square as Roger's. Twelve years older than his wife, Dan was the precinct's desk sergeant.

When the Cummings sat, Ginny said to Alice, "I heard you're taking a trip to Miami."

"I am. A municipal IT convention."

"Yeah," Dan said. "She's making a presentation on computer research." He glanced sideways at Alice. "My wife's getting quite a… reputation."

She sipped her drink, and stared straight ahead. "I've gotten the reputation because of you, old man," she muttered.

Something's off here, I thought. *Could it be the rumors our town gossip's been spreading about the reason for her recent trips are true?* When Alice leaned over and kissed Dan's cheek, I realized this was their relationship—constantly teasing each other. Plus, I had seen Alice's shows of affection for Dan.

"Really, Ally's gotten quite good at her job," Dan said, and the conversation at the table turned to the benefits of linking town and city databases into a centralized one, and eventually a single national database.

"Even without that," Alice said, "you'd be surprised at the information I have at my fingertips."

"I don't think I like that idea." Ginny Potter shuddered. "All my personal information sitting with the federal government… It would be like Big Brother's watching me."

After a few minutes, Scott Potter rose from the table. "Anyone ready for a refill?" he asked.

"Wait a sec. I'll come with you," Dan said.

A writer, I'd learned to be constantly aware and make mental notes of everything happening around me. Often, something I saw would wind up in a story I wrote. Since I had an eye on the men as they moved toward the bar, I noticed that while Dan waved to the bartender, Scott said something to him, and headed toward the door. I might have continued to watch Scott, but a moment later Alice said, "Excuse me a minute. Gotta go tinkle."

As I turned to watch her leave the bar, I got dis-tracted by a man dressed in the black pants and white shirt worn by the Echo Club servers. I leaned in his direction.

I thought Ginny must have also noticed the man, because her face took on a curious expression.

"What is it, Emlyn?" Roger asked.

"Over there, by the entrance to the Grand Ballroom. I thought I saw…" I raised my hand to point, then immed-iately lowered it. The man was gone. "It couldn't have been him."

"Who?" Roger asked.

Ginny turned her face.

"What's going on?" Dan said, as he returned to our table.

I shook my head. Ginny shrugged.

A moment later Scott and Alice came back, and our conversations resumed. I, though, was only half-focused on what the other women were saying. I couldn't stop wondering whether it had been Kevin Reinhart, my ex-husband, I'd seen. If it were, why had he come back?

After about twenty minutes, a fanfare rang from the band set up in a corner of the Grand Ballroom, and Eddie Castro, leader of The Daytrippers said, "Dinner's about to be served, folks. Come on in and find your seats."

"I'll be right there," Scott said. "Gotta check on something." He moved past the bar to the door that led to the stairwell.

Drinks in hand, Ginny, Dan and Alice hand-in-hand, Roger, and I walked into a large, rectangular room with a polished wood floor covered in part by a woven oval rug with concentric rings in shades of orange and rust. Long tables set up for family-style dining were surrounded by chairs with thin frames and vinyl seats and backs. One wall was lined by antique, oak-stained credenzas, which were used as serving stations.

At the far end of the room, near the corner in which the band played, a man with a Santa hat askew on a head with a gray military haircut, waved to us. This was Harry Woodward, head of the Niagara Falls Detective Squad. Beside him, dressed in a green and red floral skirt, and sporting a sprig of holly in her long salt and pepper braid, was Rebecca Nurse, my best friend. Owner of an arcane shop in Ellicottville, Rebecca had undertaken the task of teaching me the ways of my ancient ancestor.

Harry waived again, and pointed to chairs beside him.

We wove our way through the crowd of people attempting to find seats at the tables. When after a few minutes we made it to the seats held for us, I hugged Rebecca. I had to stand on my toes to kiss Harry's cheek. The man stood six and half feet from the ground. Even Rebecca, who was three inches taller than me, had to go tiptoe to kiss the man.

Once we had all settled at the table, Rebecca leaned toward me, and said, "I called this afternoon, but you didn't answer."

"I was at The Bon Ton, looking for something to wear tonight." I stroked the bodice of my dress. "What do you think?"

"Nice," she said, and leaned closer. "But, listen. I called you, because I read the cards this morning, and saw something—"

The Daytrippers' keyboardist started to play dinner music while pea and parmigiana soup was served.

"Tell me later," I said to Rebecca. "This smells good. Don't want it to get cold."

"Didn't get food like this in Iraq, did we, Roger?" Harry said, as he used a piece of Italian bread to sop up what was left in his bowl. A former Marine Colonel, in 2003 Harry had commanded Roger's battalion in Iraq.

"Who could think about eating over there?" Roger buttered a piece of a roll, and popped it in his mouth.

Before a conversation about military cuisine could begin, Eddie Castro took the microphone, and the band went into its version of 1D's *What Makes You Beautiful*. When the first note was sung, Harry pulled back Rebecca's chair, and they joined other couples on the dance floor.

Watching them, Roger remarked, "I didn't know the chief could dance."

I laughed. "That's because you never dated him."

"Well, I'm dating you."

"*Hmmm*, dating," I said. "Is that what the big kids call it these days?"

"I'll show you something about big kids." He pulled me from my chair. Dancing in the arms of my guy, for the moment the thought I might have seen my ex slipped from my mind.

When the band's set ended, the guitarist took a seat. While dinners of honeyed ham and turkey were served, this musician demonstrated his skill. The entree course consumed, Eddie Castro took the mic. This time, instead of announ-cing a song, he said, "Bellies full of this wonderful food, it's time for the Christmas spirit of gift-giving. Chief Woodward, wanna get this Secret Santa started?"

"Secret friggin' Santa," Scott Potter muttered. "Who came up with this bright idea?"

Dan Cummings leaned across his wife. "Happens I did, Detective. Wanted to keep everyone from goin' broke, spendin' on Christmas. Got a problem with that?"

"Uh… N-no, Sarge." Potter, whose face was a bit ruddy, turned redder, and the flush raced uphill to the horseshoe of hair that crowned his head.

"Dan's right, Scott," Ginny Potter said. "Money's so tight this year, we've gotta save where we can."

With a glance at Dan, Harry stood. The mic squeaked when he took it. Castro bent to the amplifier, and adjusted the volume, then nodded to Harry who, with a smile, announced to his fellow officers, "Even with the budget cuts, we've had another successful year in the Falls, and I want to thank each and every one of you for your tireless efforts."

Polite applause rose from the tables.

Harry held up his hand. Rubbing his stomach, he said, "Now, I might be growing round enough to be Santa Claus, but I'm not quite there yet. Still, instead of trying to squeeze down your chimneys with a bag of toys tonight—" He nodded to the hostess, who, in turn, nodded to someone in the bar. "—we have a table of Secret Santa gifts for all you great girls and boys."

A waiter at each corner, a long table covered with wrapped packages was carried into the ballroom.

"All the gifts have nametags, so find yours. Now, to everybody here, I wish you a very merry Christmas and the best of the year ahead. Before I give the microphone back to Eddie Castro, I want to give a big thank you to Lieuten-ant George Juarez for arranging this dinner."

The lieutenant stood, and bowed. Applause, raised glasses, and shouts of "Whoop!" followed.

"Now," Harry concluded, "let's see what treats the Echo Club is giving us for desert."

Ψ Ψ Ψ

Dinner over, with chattering and laughter all around us, we were settled back enjoying after-dinner drinks and coffee. Rebecca appeared a bit disheveled after spending half the night on the dance floor. I must have looked much the same. I glanced at Roger, then at Harry, and wondered, *How do these guys manage to stay so well put-together?*

As if she had read my mind—my friend seemed able to do this as easily as she read her tarot cards—she said, "Years out of the military, and it's like they're still on parade."

The guys were lost in conversation, reliving the time they'd fought together in the Middle East. Though it had been an enjoyable evening, I had not been able to remove my ex from my mind. Had it really been Kevin I saw? The more I thought about it, the more I needed to speak with someone, and that someone couldn't be Roger. He detested Kevin, and believed my ex should have been sent to prison.

Taking a deep breath, I tapped Rebecca's wrist. "Let's go to the ladies room and see if we can think up a spell that'll help how *we* look." A handy excuse to get away from our guys.

"Don't need the ladies room," she said. "Roger thinks you look great. See the way he keeps eying you? When're you gonna agree to marry him?"

I tugged at her arm, and lowered my voice to a whisper. "Come to the ladies room with me!"

She tilted her head, as if to ask a question.

"There's something I need to tell you." I yanked her from her seat, and told Roger and Harry, "Gotta do some girl stuff. We'll be back in a minute."

To reach the ladies room we had to pass through the bar, then out the door to the stairwell and up one flight. As usual after an evening of drinking, there was a line outside the ladies room. This wouldn't do. I latched onto Rebecca's arm, and pulled her back through the door to the stairwell.

"Where are you taking me?" she asked.

"I said I need to tell you something." I don't know why I whispered this. We were alone in the stairwell. "Kevin's come back."

My sleazy ex other-half was supposed to be in the federal Witness Protection Program after testifying against a gang of interstate drug dealers.

Rebecca bit her lip.

"He's here. Tonight! At least, I think I saw him sneaking around the ballroom just before we went in for dinner."

She stared at me. "I was afraid this would happen. Well, not exactly this, but something bad. That's why I phoned you this afternoon. I was thinking about you when I read the cards. I laid them out in a dawn spread. Death came up on the right— the position of the evening influence. The Devil turned up above that. You know what that means?

I had no idea what that meant.

"It means something terrible is gonna happen to-night."

"Something to do with Kevin?"

She shrugged. "I don't know. The cards are never that specific. But, if you really did see him…" She took both my hands. "Whatever happens, promise me you'll stay out of it. Please, Emlyn. For once in your life, listen to me."

I kissed her cheek, thinking, *What could be worse than what I've already seen—or worse than what my over-active writer's imagination can conjure up?*

It didn't take long to find out.

Chapter Three
Not A Creature Stirring

When we returned to the ballroom, Peter Collins was in the seat next to Roger, holding tight to the gold watch.

"I can't believe you gave me this." He rubbed the back of the watch. "All the other guys gave each other trinkets. They'll be all over me, they find out I got somethin' like this."

Roger laughed, and patted Collins's back. "Tell them it's a cheap fake, and I gave it to you so you'd remember to get to the precinct on time."

Rebecca poked her sharp elbow in my ribs, and whispered, "Tell Roger and Harry who you saw."

I shook my head.

"Tell them, or I will. Don't growl at me. I mean it, I'll tell them."

I was suddenly back in the third grade, with Mary Lou Higgins threatening to tell our teacher I'd tried to put bubble gum in her hair. As it turned out, though, neither Rebecca nor I got to tell the guys. Just then, Collins said, "You haven't opened *your* present yet, Detective Frey. What'd Santa bring you?"

The brightly wrapped package on the table in front of Roger appeared to have been opened and rewrapped. "Looks like someone else wanted to know what's in here," he said.

From a couple of seats away, Dan Cummings said, "Come on, already. Open it."

Standing behind Cummings, Scott Potter, added, "Yeah. You're the only one here that hasn't."

Alice Cummings yawned. "Dan, I'm tired," she said. "Let's go home."

Laughing, Dan replied, "In a second. I wanna see what he got."

With a soft, lady-like snort, Alice quick-stepped out of the ballroom.

"Okay, before she divorces you, I'll open it." From the size and shape of the box, it might have held a tie. Roger hefted the box. "Feels kinda heavy. Maybe I got a gold bar."

Taking my seat beside him, I watch as he undid the wrapping paper. When he opened the box, his jaw dropped.

I leaned over. "It... l-looks like a tongue."

"Gotta be a fake. Someone's idea of a joke," Harry said.

Roger held out the box.

Cummings touched the tongue. "I… think it's real."

Ginny Potter screamed.

Like an orchestra tuning up, male voices, female voices, rose from everywhere at once. Somebody near the entry to the bar shouted, "What happened?"

"Is it a fire?" someone else said.

"Someone's hurt!"

"Where—?"

"Who—?"

"What—?"

In a room full of police, their spouses or significant friends, nobody ran for the exit. After a minute during which we sat at our table and gaped at the tongue-in-a box, Harry stood.

"Everyone! Quiet!" His voice was like that of drill sergeants in movies I'd seen. "Pipe down, all of you! Sit!"

The cacophony of voices slowly faded into the sound of chairs scraping the floor.

"We seem to have an incident here," Harry said when the room at last fell silent. "I know you're getting ready to leave, but we're gonna need your patience while we figure out what's going on. So go ahead, get some more drinks. This round will be on the department."

Staring at the head table where we sat, a group of men and woman made for the bar. Others remained in their seats, urgently whispering.

Holding her long salt and pepper braid, as if it were a security blanket, Rebecca, turned to me. "I told you something bad would happen tonight. Didn't I tell you that? The cards are never wrong."

At the same time, Roger patted my leg. "Now you'll get a chance to see what real police work is about."

Queasiness in my stomach, I feared I knew what would be found at the bottom when this well got drained. Whenever my ex came into a room, trouble would walk in at his elbow. I whispered to Roger, "I need to tell you who I think I saw. It was—"

Harry interrupted me. "Not now, Emlyn." Leaning down to Roger, he said, "Detective, get Doctor Jack over here."

Roger peered around the ballroom. "Where is he?"

"You might check the bar," Dan said.

Dr. Jackson Markowitz was the county's Medical Examiner. The squad called him Doctor Jack. Because Harry's detective squad frequently consulted him, he'd been invited to this Christmas party. If the ME had a fault, it was that he drank a bit. I understood why. If *I* had to cut up the dead everyday (other than the dead I wrote about), I'd probably also frequently pop a cork.

With a nod, Roger left us. A few minutes later he returned. "Got him," he said with a grin. "Caught up with him in the bathroom."

Not surprising, I thought. *After a drink or three… or four to celebrate the season, where else would Doctor Jack be?*

A moment later, a gangly man who had a round face topped by short brown hair, came into the room with his jacket over his arm and his shirttail hanging. Though he looked nothing like a doctor, he was a good one. I'd heard him give evidence when I sat on the jury during Richard Bennet's trial.

"What have we got?" Doctor Jack said as he approached us.

Harry showed him the box. "First question, Doc. Is this real?"

Dr. Markowitz took a pair of glasses from his shirt pocket, and peered at the tongue. "*Hmm,*" he grunted. He then picked up a napkin from the table, and lifted the tongue from the box.

"Well?" Roger said.

In his deep voice that belied his slight build, the doctor said, "Appears to be."

Harry cleared his throat. "Is it human?"

The doctor closed his eyes and let out a sighing breath. "Can't be certain until I examine it thoroughly at the lab."

"Best guess?" Harry pressed.

Doctor Jack placed the box on the table, and covered it with the napkin. "You know I don't like to guess."

Harry opened his mouth to object.

The doctor raised his hand. "If you're going to hold my feet to the fire, I'd say, yes, it's human. And before you ask, it looks like it was probably severed in the last hour or two, and not by a surgical instrument."

"What cut it, then?" Scott Potter asked.

"Can't be sure. Something with a serrated blade—" He lifted a knife from the table. "Maybe like this. But, as I said, I couldn't testify to any of this. Not until—"

"Yeah, yeah," Harry said. "Not till you get this damn tongue to your lab."

I looked at Doctor Jack. "Um, how can you tell the kind of knife that was used?"

Roger shot me a narrow-eyed warning that signaled, *Emlyn, don't snoop.*

"I'm just curious," I told him. "I might be able to use something like this in a story."

I didn't get an answer. The way things seem to happen at times like this, a waitress, her face paler than her blond hair, ran in from the bar. Her eyes as wide as watermelons, she pointed, and shrieked, "Out there. The stairwell. A body!"

Once more, the dozens of police officers in the ballroom were on their feet amid a chorus of, "What?" "Who?" "Where?"

Harry immediately took command. Pointing to each in turn, he said, "Doc, Dan, Scott, with me. Roger, sit that young lady down, and find out what she knows. Lieutenant Juarez, gather up your men. See if any of 'em saw or heard something."

Dan Cummings's head swiveled in every direction. "Where's my wife? It isn't her, is it?"

Alice rushed through the door to the bar. "It's all right, Dan. I'm here. I'm okay."

"Where were you?" her husband asked, concern in his voice."

"I was in the stairwell with her." She pointed to the waitress.

Taking Alice by the elbow, Dan said, "What were you doing out there?"

She blushed, and glanced around the room. "We were… Uh, I mean, I… Oh, damn! We were having a cigarette."

Dan held her away. "You know it's illegal to smoke in public buildings."

"Talk to her about that later, Sergeant," Harry said. "Let's go!"

While Harry and his team headed through the bar to the stairwell and Lieutenant Juarez gathered his men, Roger led Alice Cummings and the waitress to the smaller Chopin Room.

I tugged Rebecca's arm. "Come on."

Grasping her wineglass, she leaned back in her chair. "Uh-uh. I'm staying out of this, and you should, too."

"But—"

"Don't give me *buts,* Emlyn. I told you what the cards said. Are you looking to maybe get killed this time?"

"I'm not going to get in the middle of this inves-tigation," I said in the most innocent tone I could muster. "I just want to hear what Alice and the waitress tell Roger. He told me I should see what police work is about. You heard him say that."

She shoved her chair further away from me. "When I was a kid in school and I told my father I hadn't told the other kids I was psychic, then swore I hadn't taken their money for reading their cards, he said to me I should never try to kid a kidder."

"Yeah. Then your father took the money you'd conned from other the kids."

She waived this off. "Don't try to kid me, Emlyn. You're gonna get involved. You can't help yourself."

I dropped my hands to my hips. "Sit there by yourself if that's what you want to do. *I'm* going to the Chopin Room."

As if searching for help, my friend's head did a 180 around the room. The police officers gathered around Lieutenant Juarez filled the far end of the ballroom. Their spouses and significant others had broken into groups on the other side.

Slowly, my friend stood. With a sigh, she said, "I can't believe you're getting me into the middle of a mess again."

"I said you can stay here," I told her, half-afraid she'd turn and sit again.

"Dammit!" she hissed as we left the ballroom. "Somebody's gotta keep you from getting killed."

Chapter Four
Not Even the Mouse

The Chopin Room was a lounge area set off from the activities in the bar and ballroom. It had a gray stone fireplace surrounded by tall windows, and maroon armchairs. By the time Rebecca and I negotiated the warren of stairs, Roger had pulled the chairs into a tight circle, and sat facing the two women. Officer Peter Collins sat off to the side, a pad and pen in his hands.

Roger glanced up as we entered the room. Though he made no remark, his expression showed disapproval.

I pulled my reluctant friend to a chair close enough to Collins that I could read what he had written. Unfortunately, his notes were in a peculiar shorthand, unreadable by anyone but him.

"Where were you before you went into the stairwell?" Roger asked Alice.

She groaned. "I already told you that. Am I a suspect, or something?"

"Not at all. I just need to get everyone's timeline straight."

With a sigh, she said, "All right. I'll tell you one more time. It was a long night. I was tired and wanted to go home, but couldn't get my husband to stop jabbering like a schoolgirl. So I picked myself up and left."

I twisted my lips. This was how she described Dan?

"And you walked through the bar— did you stop and talk to anyone?"

"No. I just wanted to get out of that place, have a cigarette, and go home."

"Why'd you go into the stairwell instead of outside to the street to wait for Dan?"

"It's cold out there, and he had the car keys. So, when I saw *her*—" Alice pointed at the waitress. "—not put on a coat when she took out a cigarette, I decided to follow her."

"Good. Now, Miss…" Roger said to the waitress.

"Abrams. Penelope Abrams." She looked at Collins. "That's P-E—"

"Thank you, Miss Abrams, that's fine. Now, at some point you went into the second floor stairwell. That was about what time?"

"Um…" She looked at her watch. "Eleven. About that time… I think."

"Good. So, about eleven you went into the stairwell to smoke—"

Her shoulders stiffened. In a pleading voice, she said, "Please don't tell my boss I did that. I could get fired."

It struck me it might be a bit late for Penelope Abrams to worry about getting fired for smoking in the building.

"I won't tell her if I don't have to," Roger said. "So, how long after you went out there did Mrs. Cummings enter the stairwell?"

With a glance at Alice, Penelope Abrams said, "When she said we could go out there, we went together."

Collins wrote a note in his pad.

"Okay. Now, when you got into the stairwell, what did you do?"

"We, uh… smoked and talked."

"For how long?"

Nervously, Abrams twisted her ring. "I don't know. Maybe five or six minutes."

Roger leaned forward. "In that five or six minutes, you didn't see a body lying there?"

The women looked at each other. "We didn't see it," Alice said.

"Not at first," Abrams agreed.

Alice picked up the thought. "But, then she spotted a pile of white tablecloths on the landing just below us, and she said if she picked them up and brought them back inside—"

"I could tell my boss I went to the stairwell to gather them for the laundry. But when I picked the first couple up, I saw…" Once more, the waitress's eyes went wide, and she grew pale. "I saw…"

"There was a man curled in the corner, and the tablecloth right on top of him had red stains." Alice clutched the other woman's hand, as if that would soften the shock of what she had seen.

Rebecca and I had been in that stairwell just a little while before these women went there to smoke, I thought. *Had that pile of tablecloths been on the landing then? Is it possible someone could have put them and the body there in only the fifteen or so minutes after we left?* I was about to interrupt Roger, and mention this possibility, but then I recalled I'd been so concerned about seeing Kevin, I wouldn't have noticed even if the tablecloths had been piled up to the ceiling.

"…I've never seen a dead person before." Abrams was saying when I again focused on her. She covered her face with her hands and sobbed.

I glanced over at Collins, who was writing in his pad with such speed, I thought he must have been trying to set a world record for shorthand.

My friend Rebecca, who had a heart as large as an elephant's, was incapable of sitting by while another human suffered. She pulled a handkerchief from her large shoulder bag, left her armchair, and knelt before Penelope Abrams. Patting the woman's eyes, she crooned, "It's okay, now. It's over. Tonight you'll sleep, and tomorrow it will be forgotten."

Roger's face tightened. He didn't believe in magic—at least, not the kind Rebecca had been teaching me—but, he wasn't one to take chances. Once the killer was caught, Penelope Abrams would have to testify at his trial. Roger did *not* want this future witness to forget what she'd seen. That he didn't immediately demand Rebecca and I leave the Chopin Room could only have been to avoid dropping the thread of his interviews. I was certain, to use a metaphor, we'd be sent to the principal's office later. At that moment, he just shook his head, and asked another question.

"Miss Abrams," he said, "did you recognize the person you saw on the landing?"

Still sobbing, the waitress shook her head.

"Did you, Alice?"

Her face turned to the tall windows, tears running down her cheeks, she responded, "I didn't, either."

From behind us, a voice called, "Identification's not gonna be a problem, Detective."

We all twisted to look at the doorway, where Harry and Scott Potter stood.

"We think we know the victim," Harry continued. "Emlyn, I thought we'd find you here. Gonna need your help to make the ID final."

A sinking feeling in my stomach, I had an idea why he'd asked me to identify the body.

Scott moved to Roger's side. Though he whispered, I sat close enough to hear him say, "It's the Mouse."

Now I was certain. Because he'd been among the shortest in our high school class, and cheese was his favorite between-meal snack, Mouse was what the kids had nicknamed my ex-husband. Hearing him referred as the Mouse now, I wondered how much that taunting name had shaped the man he'd become—a man who'd used his job selling insurance as an opportunity for blackmail. Rumor also had him scamming elderly people out of their savings with sham insurance policies. Why had I married this bottom-feeding con-artist? A good question; one I frequently asked myself—more frequently ever since Roger had decided I should marry *him*. Perhaps I had married Kevin to spite a mother who'd concocted a far different plan for my future. That was the environment from which I had grown. Recognizing this in myself evoked more sympathy for Kevin than I'd felt since he traded our marriage for an affair with a blonde bimbo. As a result, hearing he'd been murdered, I felt like I'd been punched in the stomach.

As I gasped, I heard Rebecca say, "The *Death* card in the evening influence spot... I knew something horrid would happen."

Without recognizing the cause, Roger must have seen my emotions paint a tableau on my face. He reached for my hand. "Give her a minute to collect herself, Chief," he told Harry, then led me to a far corner of the room.

"You don't have to do this, Emlyn. Not tonight," he said as he eased me into a soft leather seat. "It's just a formality. Harry knows it's him, so I can take you to the morgue in a day or two. You can make the official ID of Kevin then."

I nodded.

He kissed my forehead. "Good. I'll tell Harry."

From where I sat, I watched Harry pull Rebecca aside, and ask what she might have seen and heard. I knew she could add nothing to the investigation. She and I had been together most of the evening. If I hadn't seen or heard anything useful, she hadn't. Now I turned, and listened to Roger finish questioning Alice Cummings and Penelope Abrams.

"…I saw a couple of waiters cleaning in the bar when I came in," Abrams was saying.

"And the two bartenders?" Roger asked.

Her brow knitted, struggling to recall what she'd seen, she moved her hands in jerky motions, as if to point to each person that had been in the bar. At last, she said, "Yeah, they were there. Jeff was wiping a table by the wall, and Sonya was behind the bar, getting lemon and lime wedges into containers."

"And you, Alice?"

She approached trying to remember by closing her eyes, and moving her lips as if speaking to herself. When she finally spoke aloud, she said, "There were two… three… No, there were four that I recognized from the precinct. George Juarez was one of them. He was coming out of the bathroom when I went out to smoke.

That didn't sound right. Thinking back, I was sure I'd seen the lieutenant sitting back and nursing a drink two tables from me. *Well,* I thought, *that just proves what Roger's always telling me—witnesses are unreliable. Me, included.*

A few minutes later, Roger told the women they could leave. "Thanks for your help," he said as they stood. "Sometime next week, I like you both to stop at the precinct and sign your statements."

When the women were gone, Rebecca and I moved to where Roger and Harry were speaking with Scott Potter.

"That was interesting," Rebecca said. "I've never been interrogated in a murder investigation before."

Harry laughed. "That wasn't an interrogation. Alice Cummings and the waitress had nothing to do with killing Kevin Reinhart. They were just unlucky in finding him." He looked at us with one eye closed. "You two, on the other hand, strike me as kinda suspicious. What say, Detective, should we run 'em through the third degree?"

"Dunno, Chief," Roger said. "This Goode woman keeps telling me she knows a spell that'll have us talking in falsetto."

"*Hmm.* Well, we can have Potter here beat the info out of 'em. His wife shouldn't mind if his voice goes up an octave or two."

Scott held up his hand. "Leave me out of this. Ginny already has me singing like Frankie Valli."

"Very funny," I said. "You guys are just a riot."

"Yeah," Rebecca said. "Gonna get kind of cold sleeping by yourselves tonight."

"Yeah, tonight," Harry said, his smile gone. "Don't think Roger or I are gonna get much sleep. Gotta wrap this this crime scene up tight before we leave. You, too, Scott. Find Dan Cummings, would ya?" He reached into his jacket pocket, took out his car keys, and handed them to Rebecca. "You ladies should head out. I'll hitch a ride with Roger."

"And, Emlyn," Roger said as he helped me put on my coat. "Go to bed. Stay out of this."

Stay out of it? Right. After this night, I was more than ready to go home, but not to bed. Someone I knew and once thought I cared about had been murdered. Who had killed him? I wanted to start figuring that out. My way.

Chapter Five
Stockings Hung By The Chimney With Care

"I just need to get a clue as to why Kevin was at the Echo Club," I said as Rebecca and I came through my front door.

My house didn't have a chimney—my father feared putting one in would create a fire hazard—so I had tacked Christmas stockings for Roger, me, and my cat on the wall near the front door. Those stockings had grown a bit fatter each day since I'd hung them.

From the hall, I saw Elvira's head lift from the armrest of my oversized wingback chair. Until this hefty albino feline adopted me and my home, this was my favorite chair, the one in which I would sit, and read, and watch the seasons change outside the French door. The cat let out a sharp *meeeow,* which I took to mean, *How about less noise? I'm trying to sleep!*

I took off my coat, and hung it and Rebecca's in the hall closet. When I closed the door, I said, "Forget sleep, cat. We have a puzzle to solve."

"No we don't! You heard Roger." Rebecca dropped her shoulder bag on my dinette table. "I'm gonna make us some herbal tea. It'll help you sleep. I'll bet by the time you wake up, the guys will have arrested whoever killed Kevin."

Elvira leaped from her chair. In an instant she was at my feet, looking up with an expression that asked, *Somebody finally offed that slimebucket? Gotta find who did it, give him a medal!* From the moment she'd met my ex, Elvira abhorred him.

I bent over and stared at her. "Did *you* kill him?"

The cat huffed, threw up her head, and sauntered back to her nest in my chair.

"Oh, give me a break," Rebecca said as she carried two mugs of tea from the kitchen. "Your cat killed Kevin?"

I followed her into the living room. "Well… but, see that's my point. So many people at the Echo Club tonight—guests and staff. There has to be at least a dozen or more that knew him. And, if they knew him, they probably hated him enough to want him dead. With that many suspects, it'll be weeks before Roger and Harry come close to figuring out the person who actually did it. By then, the killer will be long gone."

"Maybe yes, maybe no. But, Emlyn, catching him isn't *your* problem." She placed the mugs on the coffee table. Spreading her skirt, she sat on the sofa and crossed her legs.

I remained standing in the center of the room. "You're right," I said. "It's not my *problem*. But, see, it's like a puzzle, and you know how I love those."

I did love puzzles—of any kind. On Saturdays, the *Buffalo News* had a Word Jumble, a Sudoku, and a reprint of a Sunday *New York Times* crossword. On that day, a story I might be writing got set aside until I'd solved them all. My eyes rolling back from the pleasure brought by the thought, I said, "If it weren't that we're talking about Kevin getting *murdered*, I'd feel like Santa had brought me a Christmas present."

Rebecca sat up straight with her lips twisted. "You need to get a new hobby. You know that?"

My cat lifted her head, and mewed, as if to say, *I love Emlyn's hobby.*

"Don't encourage her, Elvira," Rebecca said. "God. You're as bad as she is!"

As if the idea of a puzzle to unravel had a *use by date* that suddenly expired, my pleasure faded. "Listen to me," I said. "There isn't a thing I can do to save Kevin, but I can at least find out who killed him. I'm good at solving that kind of puzzle."

"Yeah. You're also good at almost getting us both killed."

"Rebecca, somebody murdered the man I was once married to, cut out his tongue. You can't expect me to sit here and do nothing about it."

Groaning, she said, "I know you feel bad about him." She patted the seat next to her. "Come, sit down. Drink your tea while it's still hot. Tomorrow's Christmas…" She looked over at the railroad clock hung on the wall above my bookcases. "*Today* is Christmas. Go to bed. When you see all the presents you'll get to open in the morning, you'll change your mind about getting involved in this."

At one time a lakeside cottage, my house had been redone by my father, who had been a carpenter, so that it now had what interior decorators call an open floorplan. This meant everything on the ground floor—including the kitchen—could be seen from everywhere. An étagère marked the break between my living and dining rooms. In the living room, next to the sofa, my bookcases were in the corner adjacent from my desk, near enough to grab a reference when needed. That Christmas day I didn't want a reference work from my bookcase. Turning my back on Rebecca, I reached into my top desk drawer where I kept a special book. Written by Sarah Goode more than 300 years ago, this was my ancient relative's *Book of Shadows*, a diary of a sort, in which she recorded her private thoughts and, uh… recipes she'd used in connection with the craft for which she'd been hanged.

Carrying the old book to the sofa, I told Rebecca, "We can sleep later. Right now I want to see if something Sarah wrote will give me an idea as to who killed Kevin."

I never claimed anything in this book could solve a crime—at least, not directly. However, several times an observation Sarah had made about the people that populated Salem in 1692 gave me a hint as to the motive of someone I knew in Niagara Falls.

The book in my hand, I sat next to Rebecca. "Help me with this?" I said. The book, with its brittle pages, and faded words spelled in a way nobody alive spelled them any longer, was difficult to read. As a result, I used a magnifying glass to help me decipher old Sarah's hand-writing.

My friend gritted her teeth.

"Come on," I said to her. "You want to go to bed? The sooner you help me read this, the sooner I'll let you."

Elvira raised her head, glared as us, and growled. It was as if she said, *Help her already so I can get some sleep!*

Rebecca picked up one of the sofa's throw pillows, and hurled it at my cat. "You're as impossible at she is!"

I didn't mind being called impossible. It meant I'd won. My house a bit chilly at this late hour, I tucked the gray afghan my grandmother had knitted over my lap and Rebecca's, then took the magnifying glass from the coffee table, and opened the book. While Rebecca watched a sprinkle of snow through the panes of the French door, I scanned down one page then another, until an entry Sarah Goode had written on December 21, 1691 caught my attention. Aloud, I read:

*"The days grow now as cold as the hearts that rule this Salem Town (*Sarah spelled it Towne*). Five years has it been since the law of stiff reverends proclaiming their holiness was forgotten. Still their voices and sermons are recalled. No longer a five pence fine—a mighty sum in this hard time—if one is found to celebrate the yuletide, but the punishment is worse still. It is fear of years long shunning, withholding of Christian charity that silences celebration. Might it be that, as in Old*

Testament births, a twin child also was born in that manger, one that grew to preach fear? No fear, but joy alone should there be while the earth sleeps in these days of the winter solstice. In my girlhood, I recall wassailing with friends, begging a small gift for the season's goodwill. But, oh, 'twas another place and time. This Salem is not London. Here do men, and it is rumored even a woman or two, lock their doors and drink while plotting what they might take that is not theirs.

"I cannot hide away at a time such as this, but will celebrate as the Old Ones did before plots and deception stole from them this yule joy. In an old barn at Salem's edge will I adorn an altar in pine, rosemary, and juniper, and mark my altar in a circle of stones. Into my cast-iron pot will I place a red candle and around it burn incense..."

"What do you think, Rebecca? Is a clue hidden in there?" I said when, my throat dry, I paused for a sip of tea.

Her response was a soft, fluttering snore. I glanced over at my sleeping friend. "So much for you helping me," I muttered. "At least you're listening, cat."

Elvira's snoring was louder than Rebecca's.

"I'll just do this myself, then," I told Sarah's book. Fascinated by the solstice rite she'd written of, and certain something within this entry would lead my mind to who killed Kevin, I would have continued to read all night, if necessary. I didn't, though, because my front door opened, a gust of wind rushed in, and a voice carried by that stiff breeze, said, "We're home. Are you guys still awake?"

Chapter Six
Hoping St. Nicholas Soon Would Be There

It wasn't the jolly old elf that followed the voice into my house, but Roger and Harry. In an instant, Rebecca's eyes opened and she was off the sofa.

"So much for you being asleep, pal," I grumbled. I yawned, and stretched.

Roger came from the hall, and tossed his navy blue overcoat onto the back of my overstuffed wingback chair. The skirt of the coat sagged over Elvira's head. Snarling, she snapped her body until the coat fell to the floor.

"Sorry 'bout that." Roger reached down to scratch between the cat's ears before stooping to retrieve his coat.

Elvira followed his movements with an expression I can describe only as adoration. Had I buried Elvira in *my* coat, she would have hissed at me, then stomped off in a huff. Of course, I wasn't a six-foot-one male with the kind of rugged face that could drive even a female feline to distraction.

Roger read my expression—the man knew me well. His lips pursed, he said, "Oh, are you a little jealous, dear?" He moved to the sofa, bent over me, and scratched my forehead.

I growled. I would have stomped off in a huff if I hadn't been tangled in the wool afghan. I took a deep breath, and sighed when it struck me that, in living with this albino creature, instead of the cat taking on my character, I'd begun to take on hers. I hadn't behaved this way before she showed up at my door… Had I?

While I gnawed on this thought, Harry and Rebecca came from the kitchen, each carrying two white mugs.

"After the night you've had, I thought you could use this," Rebecca said as she handed a mug to Roger.

I hadn't thought to do this for my guy, she had. What was wrong with me? How could Roger have fallen in love with a witch such as me? Sitting, staring at the mug of freshly brewed tea Rebecca now handed me, I thought perhaps this understanding might be the gift Santa intended I receive this Christmas. When I glanced up, the darn cat was ginning at me. It was as if she saw the direction in which my thoughts had wandered, and approved of it.

"'Oh Lord that lends me life, lend me a heart replete with thankfulness,'" I said.

The cat tilted her head. Clearly, she hadn't read Shakespeare's Henry the Sixth. Frankly, I hadn't, either. This was a quote I'd found while doing research. Still the sentiment was there, and when Roger sat beside me, I leaned over, threw my arms around his neck, and kissed him.

When I, at last, released him, with a broad smile he asked, "What was that for?"

"Merry Christmas," I said.

From her perch on Harry's lap, Rebecca said, "Does this mean you'll finally marry him?"

Roger's head tilted and his smile grew.

I gasped. My friend's question and my guy's ex-pression were one-two punches that landed in the gut of my fear. The path Kevin had followed was probably what got him killed. It had been a long time since I felt anything but disgust for him, yet learning of his murder hurt. Roger's career was far more dangerous. How much more would it hurt if this *good* man I loved were killed? I needed to give this subject a wide berth.

I picked up Sarah Goode's book, and cleared my throat. "I hoped I could get a clue to what happened tonight in here."

Rebecca lifted her head and rolled her eyes.

Roger loved me enough to let me off the hook—at least, for now. "Did you find something?" he asked.

"She didn't," Rebecca said.

Attack was a good defense. Before my friend could swing us back to the uncomfortable subject of marriage, I said, "How would you know? You were asleep." Then, to make sure we stayed on the right road, I asked Harry, "Did you learn anything at the Echo Club?"

"Afraid not," he said. "All the staff I spoke to are covered. Working in pairs, none of 'em were alone long enough to pull off a killing and a body dump. What about you, Detective? That Abrams waitress clear?"

I breathed a sigh of relief. The formality of Harry's response moved us so far from the mountain of marriage, stubborn Rebecca would need a Sherpa guide to bring us back.

"She's clear, too, Chief," Roger said. "Other staff saw her enough that the only time she was alone was the minute before Alice Cummings caught up with her."

"So who does that leave?" I asked.

Harry clicked his tongue. "I don't like it, but it only leaves our people."

Rebecca twisted on his lap to look at him. "A *cop* murdered Kevin?"

We fell silent as this unthinkable possibility sunk in.

After a minute, Harry eased Rebecca from his lap, and stood. "Gotta be another answer. Maybe if I sleep on it, it'll come to me." To Roger, he said, "Mind if Becca and I bunk at your house tonight?"

"Not a problem, Chief. In fact, I'll come with you. There's a…" He glanced in my direction. "…a few things I wanna pick up."

I knew he didn't need a change of clothes. My gifts for him were already under the tree.

Ψ Ψ Ψ

Left alone, just me and the cat, I wasn't ready to, as Clement Moore's poem goes, settle in for a long winter nap. I refused to believe in the possibility of a perfect crime. Someplace the killer had to have made a slip. A moment when he was where he shouldn't have been, a misplaced word. The mistake would not be apparent, but there would be one. I was determined to find it. I just needed a place to start. Was there a word or a phrase I'd read in Sarah's book that would point toward that place?

My thoughts were interrupted when I heard the opening measures of Rick Gaunt's song, *Niagara Falls*. Startled, I looked around my living room. The song played again. This was clearly a cellphone ringtone, but not mine. A third time the song played, and now I spotted the source. It came from an older flip-style phone I recognized as belonging to Harry. He must have put it on the lamp table when Rebecca sat on his lap. I laughed. At this very late hour, he must be calling his phone to learn where he'd left it.

Leaning over, I picked up the phone, flipped it open, and said, "Yes, Harry, you left your phone at my house."

"Emlyn?" The surprised voice wasn't his.

"Uh, yeah?"

"It's Ginny, uh… Ginny Potter. Is Chief Woodward there?"

I held the phone away, and looked at it. Why was she calling Harry at this hour of the night? "The chief isn't here. He went next door, and left his phone at my house."

"Oh…" From the way she uttered the single word, I got the impression something worried her.

"Can I help you, Ginny?" I said. "Is there a problem?"

"I… don't know. I'm here with Alice Cummings. Do you know where our husbands are?"

"I don't. I can only think they're finishing up at the Echo Club." I didn't know if they were, but it made sense.

"Thanks, Emlyn." It sounded as though she took a breath. "Yeah, that's probably where they are."

"Only, they aren't answering their phones." Alice Cummings said this. Ginny had probably set her phone so they could both hear and talk. "After what happened tonight, we were worried. I mean, a killer roaming around, and all."

"It *was* horrible, wasn't it? The body they found is… was my ex-husband," I said.

"Does the chief have an idea who did it—killed him, I mean?" Ginny asked.

"If he does, he didn't tell me. That's a cop for you, always so closed-mouth."

I heard them both giggle nervously. Then I heard what sounded like someone inhaled deeply, and quickly exhaled. This had to be Alice lighting a cigarette.

"But you know, now that we're talking about it, I remembered something I meant to tell Harry and Roger. That thief that Scott mentioned before dinner—the one that robbed the jewelry store?"

"Derek Street?" Alice asked.

"Yes. Before Kevin went into witness protection, he and Street ran around together."

"You didn't tell the chief?" Ginny said.

"By the time he and Roger got here, I'd forgotten to mention it. It's all right, though. He'll be here in the morning. I can tell him then."

We spoke for another few minutes, then Alice said, "Oh. Our husbands just got here."

"Thanks for taking our minds off worrying about them, Emlyn," Ginny said.

When she turned off her phone, I thought, *A con-nection between Derek Street and Kevin. Could that be the starting point I need?*

Still snuggled under my grandmother's wool cover, I picked up my magnifying glass, and the mug of tea Rebecca had brewed. Certain something in what old Sarah had written would give me an idea as to why a connection with Street might have gotten Kevin killed—this had happened more than once before—I returned to her book and the entry I'd been reading before Roger and Harry came home.

...these words I chanted: I light this fire in your honor, Mother Goddess. With

this candle do you bring light from the dark, warmth from cold, life from death. While these words did I sing, like an eagle in summer my thoughts flew to the fine house of Reverend Parris, empty as this yuletide nears. Long weeks has he, in a stern Puritan voice, preached the evil of riotous wassailing as Satan's song. Yet, this day has his family fled to New Amsterdam—called after the noble York these past twenty-seven years—there to wassail undetected...

As I read this, the magnifying glass slipped from my hand, and I yawned. I glanced at the mug from which I had been sipping. The tea... brewed by Rebecca... it would help me sleep, she had said...

I don't know how long Roger had been gone or how late he returned. I recall hearing the wind howl, and thinking it might be a harbinger of a white Christmas. Then, I was aware of nothing until I felt a gentle kiss on my lips, and heard Roger say, "We've had a long day, my love. It's time we cuddle up."

My eyes half open, I saw the brown flecks dance in his hazel eyes. Wrapping my arms around his neck I pulled him close, and gave him a long, slow kiss. Our lips still together, he lifted me from the sofa. This man was strong, and loyal. As he carried me up the stairs, if he again asked me to marry him, I might have said yes. On my bed, he undressed me, and for the next hour or so, gave me a better Christmas gift than any he might have put under my tree.

The rest of the night we snuggled warm in my bed.

Chapter Seven
Out On The Lawn, I heard Such A Clatter

Sunlight broke through my bedroom window. When I rolled over, the digital display on my clock read 9:33. I stretched, then climbed from under the quilt. Careful not to wake Roger—the man worked long hours, and deserved to sleep-in once in a while—I moved to the other side of the bed. Holding back my hair, I kissed his cheek. When I turned, I saw Elvira peeing through the half-closed bedroom door. Staring at me, she fluffed her body and licked her lips, sending me the silent message, *It's about time you woke up. I'm a growing cat. I need to be fed.*

I looked down at my hefty beast, and thought, *Just look what you're growing into.* I didn't say it, though. Christmas morning was not a time to be snippy. With a smile, I told the cat, "Food's coming up right now."

If cats can't smile—they don't have the facial muscles necessary to do it—why did it looked as if mine did? Her eyes wide, she spun, and scooted from my room.

The horror of last night laid aside, at least for the moment, I started downstairs. Yesterday afternoon I'd prepared a breakfast casserole—egg bread, eggs, half-and-half, sausage and three kinds of cheese. All it needed was a half hour of oven-time before it would be ready for my guy. I was pleased Rebecca and Harry were next door. I'd made more than enough to share with them.

When I reached the bottom step, I head a knock on my door. Certain it was Rebecca who stood on my stoop, with a beaming smile, I turned the knob.

Just as I pulled the door open, a rumbling in my driveway caused me to freeze. When this was followed by the sound of metal hitting metal, I fell backward onto the step, my face buried in my hands. I reacted this way, because times I had gotten involved in a murder case, the killer had come after me. Once a bottle-bomb had been tossed through my window, another time my car had been blown to nuts and bolts. Oh, and let's not forget the man with a gun in my living room. You'd think after all this I would have learned to stay safely tucked in my bed when a killer was on the loose. But, no. As my mother used to say, "Emlyn, you never learn!"

The door swung open, but instead of coming in, Rebecca leaned from the doorway and stared back toward Roger's house. Over her shoulder, she asked, "Why are you having your driveway plowed? There wasn't more than a half-inch of snow last night." She stepped back onto the stoop. "The guy on the plow smashed Harry's bumper!"

"My driveway plowed?" I stood, moved to the door, and looked past her. "I didn't... Roger's the only one that plows my driveway." Wrapping my robe around me, I pushed past Rebecca. A step from my door stoop, I shouted, "Hey! What are you doing?"

At the same time, Harry ran from Roger's house, and called, "You there. Hold on!"

I took a step toward the four-by-four pushing the plow, but stopped when the passenger-side window rolled down. Something was off. Truck windows weren't tinted this dark.

"You there!" Harry again called.

From behind me, I heard Roger say," What's going on here?"

The next thing I heard was the crack of gunfire. The bullet pinged off the cement stoop—I saw a chip of cement fly up. I heard a second shot. I had no idea what this bullet hit. I didn't care. It didn't hit me. With Roger and Harry both rushing toward the four-by-four, the shooter must have rushed his shots.

I dove onto the quarter inch of snow on my lawn, covering my head with my hands. In that position, I heard gears grind, and Roger and Harry shouting. I couldn't make out what they said.

I had no idea how long I stayed face down in the snow. I suspect it was no more than a minute before Rebecca grabbed my arm, and yelled, "Get up. Get inside. Fast!"

I moved. Not because my friend yanked me to my feet, and pushed me. Sheer animal instinct for survival propelled me up the stoop and through my front door. Here, though, was the problem: blinded by my instinct for flight, I failed to take note of my condition and that of the floor I ran onto. A damp polished wood floor in my hall, packed snow on my socks… This nearly accomplished what the shooter hadn't. When I tried to stop, my body performed what ice skaters might call an attempt at a double Axel—a completely failed attempt. As soon as I entered the house, I skidded on the floor. I tried to grab onto the kitchen doorframe. This threw me into a tumbling spin. I banged against the stools in front of the kitchen counter, slid onto the living room carpet, and hit the coffee table with my back. I lay there, stunned and moaning.

When I, at last, could focus, I saw Rebecca kneeling beside me, her hand on my chest. "Don't try to move," she said.

Elvira, on her haunches, licked my face.

From the front door, Roger shouted, "What hap-pened?" Footsteps pounded down the hall. "Tell me she wasn't hit!" He dropped to his knees beside me, checking my torso, arms, and legs for gunshot wounds.

A moment later, I heard the front door open then close. "They got away," Harry said. "Not even a plate on the damn truck—" He must have seen Rebecca, Roger, and the cat ministering to me. "No, no!" he shouted. Again running feet came into the living room.

"I don't see any bleeding," Roger said.

"She wasn't shot. She slipped when she ran into the house," Rebecca told him.

I shook my head, trying to clear my mind. "I'm o-okay…" I wiggled my fingers, and shook my hands. "…I think. Let me get up."

"You're sure?" Roger said.

I nodded.

His hand on my back, he helped me to my feet.

So far, so good, I thought. Then I straightened up, and a bolt of electricity shot from my ankles to the base of my skull. Whimpering, I dropped to my hands and knees.

"Take her to the sofa!" Harry said.

"No. Get her upstairs, and into dry clothes." Rebecca said. "She's shivering."

Until that second, I hadn't felt the cold or realized my teeth were chattering.

"Becca might be right," Harry said. "While you do that, I'm gonna get Crime Scene over here, see if they can get a clue to who the shooter was."

"Good idea," Roger said. "I wanna get my hands on that guy."

Harry rubbed his fist. "Can't blame you, Detective. Wrecked our Christmas. I'd like to hang him from the top of a tree."

I didn't remind him that an angel or a star was placed on top of a Christmas tree, and whoever had taken shots at me was neither.

"Let me know what Crime Scene finds," Roger said, and wrapped his arms around me. Rebecca and the cat following him up the stairs, he carried me to my bedroom.

He pulled pajamas from a drawer built into my platform bed and a bathrobe from my closet. Rebecca helped me to the bathroom, undressed me, and held me while I stood, stooped, under a hot shower. In a minute or two my shivering stopped, and I was able to straighten up a bit. After she helped me dry off, wrapped in a bath sheet and leaning on my friend, I made it back to my room.

"Looks like the shower helped," Roger said when he saw me standing more erect. From the way his eyes roamed over my body, I had the impression he liked seeing me dressed in nothing but the towel.

My cat apparently noticed his expression. With a snort, she jumped on my bed, and curled up.

"You probably just a pulled a muscle," Rebecca said to me as she inspected the bright green and red plaid pajamas Roger had selected, and the mauve and white stripped bathrobe. Shaking her head, she returned the robe to the closet, and took out my solid green flannel housecoat. "Much better."

Roger pressed his fingers on my lower back. Though his touch was gentle, I winced. "I'm thinking this is more than just a muscle pull. Tomorrow morning I'm taking you to Dr. Arnold. For now, you'd better rest in bed."

I glared at him. "On Christmas day? Uh-uh. Not gonna happen. Help me down the stairs. I've got a casserole ready for the oven."

It wasn't just the brunch casserole I had on my mind. I knew Roger and Harry would spend the day talking about the shots fired at me this morning, and how that might tie together with Kevin's murder at the Echo Club last night. I intended to take part in that conversation.

Roger sighed and shook his head. A wise man, he knew better than to engage in an argument when my voice was this firm.

Rebecca, who also knew me well, turned her back and headed for my bedroom door. As she opened it, she said, "I'll put the food in the oven. You carry her downstairs."

"Set the timer for thirty minutes," I called after her.

Elvira looked up at me, and let out a long *meeeow*. It was as if the cat said, *Your mother was right. You don't ever learn.*

Chapter Eight
Now Dasher, Now Dancer, Now Prancer, Now Vixen

It turned out I'd put together a casserole large enough to feed the five of us (Elvira preferred the egg casserole to her cat food), plus the three members of the Crime Scene Unit that arrived at my house.

"This food almost makes it worth volunteering for duty today," one of the team members told me.

The unit found little to report. Though my next door neighbors, the Nelsons, heard the shots, by the time they looked out their window the four-by-four was gone. No one else at home on River Road had seen or heard anything. One piece of evidence *had* been recovered.

"Can't tell for sure, Chief," the team leader said when he showed Harry the evidence bag, "but it looks like the slug we dug out of Emlyn's doorframe could be one of ours."

A deep frown on his face, Harry told the man to get ballistics on it immediately. "If this is one of ours, I'm wanting to know whose pistol it came from post-haste."

Apparently, the department maintained a file on each weapon issued.

Brunch eaten, Rebecca gathered our plates, and took them to the sink.

"I can clean up in here," I protested.

"Uh-uh," Roger said. "You need to stay off your feet till I get you to your doctor and we find out what you did to you back." With that, he lifted me from the kitchen chair.

Harry remained in the kitchen to dry the dishes Rebecca washed. During the entire task, I heard him grumble that he refused to believe an officer or one of his detectives could have stabbed "that damned Mouse, Kevin Reinhart, and sliced off his tongue."

In the living room, Roger set me on the sofa and covered me with my grandmother's afghan. Picking up the television remote, he changed channels until *The Bishop's Wife* appeared on the screen. In this film, Cary Grant, a wingless angel, is sent to save David Niven's marriage to Loretta Young. Though this was one of my favorite Christmas movies, my mind refused to become lost in the story. While I leaned against Roger's shoulder, the scene I saw continually flashed between the Echo Club last night and my front lawn this morning, and my eyes moved from the TV screen to

Sarah Goode's *Book* of *Shadows* on my coffee table.

There's an answer in something Sarah wrote about Christmas, I thought. I mentally replayed her December 21, 1691 entry. *Reverend Parris. Leaving Salem to wassail in New York.* Like a tiny white Christmas angel, the solution fluttered its wings just in front of me. I reached for it…

"What are you doing?" Roger said. "Sit still."

Instead of mentally reaching for the answer, I'd actually clutched at the air.

"I was…" I felt my cheeks burn. "Uh, I thought…"

He kissed my forehead. "Watch the movie."

The man was so transparent. This was a story about love and marriage. My mind yanked back to the subject I'd been avoiding for months, I watched the tiny angel flutter out of reach. Just as I again grabbed for the angel—only mentally, this time—Harry stormed into the living room.

"Dammit!" he said. "I refuse to believe one of ours would do something like this."

Trailing behind him, Rebecca said, "Calm down. You'll give yourself a stroke."

My cat seemed to always sense disaster about to strike. This day, her sixth sense saved her a trip to the animal hospital. As Harry neared her, she woke from her morning nap, and leaped from my overstuffed wingback chair just before his very large body dropped into it. A running step, and she jumped up on the coffee table, and sprang onto my chest. What small grip I had on the clue to Kevin's killer got swamped by the tidal wave of pain that rushed up from my lower back. My reaction, an abrupt doubling over, tossed the cat to floor next to the overstuffed chair. There she sat with an expression as stunned as mine.

Rebecca's head turned from me to the cat and back to me. "I've got something that'll ease the pain, Emlyn."

The cat shook her body, and looked up at my friend with an expression that I think said, *Hey, what about my pain?* I couldn't be sure about her expression, though, since my pain still had my eyes crossed.

"Yes, Elvira, this will take care of you, too." Rebecca glanced at me.

Though I didn't know what form it would take, I had a pretty good idea what she had in mind. "Kitchen utility drawer," I said.

She went to the kitchen, and returned in less than a minute, holding up a key. I nodded, and said, "Second shelf."

She moved toward the front door. In the hall, she opened the door to my basement, and went down. During this entire exchange, Harry had stared at me. Now he said, "Are you two psychic?"

My back pain having subsided enough, I was able to laugh. Though we weren't psychic, there were times my friend and I could speak to each other without words. In this instance, I knew she intended to use the 'old ways' to ease my pain. While she wouldn't set up an altar and conduct a ritual to accomplish this, not with Roger and Harry present, she needed certain material to work a spell. Though some of the things she needed could be found in my kitchen—a dish, a knife, dried herbs—the everyday use of those things made them mundane. For her spell, Rebecca required material reserved for use in the ways of the Old Ones. These things I kept locked in my basement tool cabinet.

I heard Rebecca's hurried footsteps on the basement stairs. When she returned to my living room, she was holding a silver plated dish, an athame, a stick of incense, a small jar of ground cinnamon, and another jar of dried thyme. She placed these near me on the coffee table. "God of the sun," she said. "Bringer of warmth in the cold, I light this in your honor." She tapped the athame on the incense, then lit the incense in the dish. "Goddess of the moon, mother of the gods, you who comfort your children, ease this one's pain." She sprinkled the cinnamon and thyme over the lit incense.

Roger shook his head. "Do you two really think incense and prayers will help? Tomorrow, the doctor will fix Emlyn's back." At one time or another I might have mentioned that my guy believes magic is only slight-of-hand performed by stage magicians.

Almost immediately, the tight muscles in my back relaxed. Turning my head up to look at him, I said, "After all this time we've been together, I think you would've learned herbs and spices can do all kinds of things. In fact, I already feel a little better."

"Yeah, well… That could've happened, because you believe the hocus pocus you do works."

I looked down at my cat. She was curled up, snoring, at Harry's feet. Clearly, the incense also made her feel better.

Rebecca pulled a dining room armchair next to Harry. Sitting, she gave Roger her best Mona Lisa smile. "Maybe it's just a psychological effect… But, you never know."

"Uh-huh. Then since you're feeling better, Emlyn, how about opening your presents?" I knew my guy. He changed the subject to avoid admitting Rebecca and I might be right.

Harry, who'd been spending all of his off-time with Rebecca, had been silent during this give-and-take—probably because things he'd seen in her shop had caused him to consider the possibility that, as Shakespeare wrote, not everything in heaven and on earth is explainable. When Roger suggested I see what he'd bought me for Christmas, Harry grumbled, "The only gift *I* want this year is to have whoever shot at Emlyn locked in a cell." He turned to Rebecca. "Do you have a spell to accomplish that?"

I slid up against Roger's chest. "Actually, I know a clairvoyance—"

Roger laid his hand on my wrist. "Don't get started with this, Emlyn. It's—"

"Yes, I know." Like a schoolgirl reciting a boring lesson, in a monotone, I said, "It's police legwork, not magic, that solves cases."

For mocking him, I received a light slap on my wrist. "Since you know that, you'll stay out of this and let me and Harry do our job."

"He's right. Amateurs get hurt, getting involved with murders." Harry looked hard at me. "Plus, it's more worrisome when you drag my lady into the danger."

My rat-fink friend, Rebecca, nodded.

"Fine, I'll stay out of this," I said. "And I won't tell you what I remembered." Sulking this way was, I admit, childish. It did, though, elicit the needed response.

Roger sighed. "Okay, what did you remember?"

"It has to do with that robbery you and Scott Potter were talking about before dinner last night." In a few words, I told them about the phony life insurance scam my ex and Derek Street had run.

"Why didn't you tell us about that when they were doing it?" Harry demanded.

"I only found out about the scam after Kevin went into witness protection." I turned to Roger. "And it was only a rumor. All I knew for certain was that Street and Kevin used to hang out together at Flannery's Bar on Pine Avenue."

"Okay," Harry said. "I'll have Detective Potter check into that. It might mean more charges against Street. But, how does that help us in this case. Couldn't be Street that murdered Reinhart and took shots at you. The guy's locked up tight."

"I don't know. It's just that Scott Potter said he's sure Street had a partner in the Firth jewelry store robbery, and since he and Kevin used to be…" I shrugged.

"That kind of makes sense," Roger said. "But that still doesn't tell us who killed Reinhart.

Rebecca looked from Roger to Harry. "Maybe Derek Street bribed a guard or something, and got out for the night."

"Can't be," Harry said. "If he did that, he'd have to still be out to take shots at Emlyn. If he was, the county lockup would've called to tell Scott that Street escaped."

We sat in silence for a minute or two, until Roger asked, "Emlyn, who else knows about the connection between Reinhart and Street?"

I closed my eyes, trying to recall who had told me about the connection. "I think it must have been… No. I'm *sure* I heard it from Grace Linden. We were in the Bella Vita hair salon when she told me." Gossip-Grace had a shopping bag filled with the secrets of half the people in Niagara Falls (each time I saw her, wondering what she knew about me made me shudder).

Harry ran a hand over his gray military-cut hair. "That gets us nowhere. If Linden told you, she could've told dozens of people. Plus, how many people at Bella Vita heard her tell you?"

"Wait a second," Rebecca said. "Have you thought that maybe killing Kevin Reinhart and shooting at Emlyn might not be connected?"

Though Elvira looked to be asleep, she must have been listening to us. As soon as Rebecca asked her question, the cat raised her head from her paws, and meowed. It sounded like she said, *Yeah, who else has Emlyn ticked off lately?*

The cat was lucky fear of the back pain returning made me afraid to move. Had I not been, I might have thrown the sofa at her.

Roger shook his head. "No. Shooting at Emlyn so soon after the murder last night—the two things have to be connected."

Grabbing this line of thought, Harry said, "That can only mean the killer wanted to keep Emlyn from telling us about Reinhart and Street." His shoulders slumped and his lips turned down into a puzzled frown. "But, why pick now to try and silence her—a time he had to know you'd be around, Roger?"

"Desperation." Roger sat up straight, certain he had the answer. "He must've only just found out about the Reinhart/Street connection." He leaned over my shoulder to look at me. "Did you tell anyone at the Echo Club about it after the body was found?"

"I was only with Rebecca after Kevin…" I stopped, remembering. "Wait. No. After you all went next door last night, Ginny Potter called your phone, Harry. Alice Cummings was with her. They were worried because their husbands still hadn't gotten home. We talked for a few minutes about what had happened, and I mentioned remem-bering about Kevin and Street. Ginny asked whether I'd told you about it, and I said I'd forgotten to. But, because you were next door, Harry, I'd tell you in the morning… But, Ginny and Alice, why would either of them kill Kevin?"

"Good question," Harry said. "Here's another one. Where were Cummings and Potter when their wives called? They left the club the same time we did."

"You don't think it was one of them?"

I understood Roger's concern. Dan Cummings, an older officer just a year away from retirement, was his friend. Scott Potter was a detective he'd worked with.

"That's what I want to find out. If their wives were the only ones that just learned Emlyn knew about Reinhart's connection with Street, and if they told their husbands…" He patted his jacket pocket. "Where's my cellphone?"

"On the lamp table next to you." I pointed. "You forgot it when you went to Roger's house last night."

Harry picked up the phone, and punched in seven numbers. "Lieutenant Juarez? This is Chief Woodward. You're on duty today?" He laughed. "Yeah, I hear what you're saying about short straws. Listen, I need you to get hold of Detective Potter and Sergeant Cummings, ask 'em to meet me at the precinct in an hour… Yeah, I know it's Christmas day. Just do it, please. Tell 'em it has to do with the Reinhart case. Say we might've caught a break."

"You're going to work today?" Rebecca sounded a little hurt. This was the first Christmas she and Harry would be spending together. My friend had just gotten a lesson in what it meant to be dating a cop.

Harry leaned over and kissed her. "Sorry, Becca. Gotta do this. Don't expect I'll be more than a couple of hours."

Roger slid from the sofa.

"Where are you going, Detective," Harry asked.

"With you, of course."

"Uh-uh. You need to stay here with Emlyn, in case the shooter thinks of making another try at her."

Elvira looked at Harry with an expression that might have said, *He can go with you. I'll protect Emlyn.* I had a good reason for reading this in my cat's expression. When a former rock and roll icon had been murdered, this cat had put herself in harm's way to protect me from the killer.

Chapter Nine
Dash Away! Dash Away! Dash Away All!

When Harry left, Roger returned to the sofa, and picked up the TV remote. "Steelers are playing the Ravens," he said. "Odds makers say this'll be a good game."

So much for spending the day watching Christmas movies.

"Men and their football," Rebecca muttered. She took the cinnamon powder from the coffee table, and her ten gallon-size shoulder bag from the white Formica counter that separated my living room from the kitchen. "I don't know about you two," she said. "I could use some tea."

Elvira stood, shook her body, and followed my friend.

"You can't be hungry," I said to the cat. "Not after eating so much of my casserole."

She looked over her shoulder at me and snorted.

From the kitchen, Rebecca leaned over the counter. "Do you have any lavender?"

"What are going brew now?" I asked.

"A cinnamon and lavender tea—I taught you this. It'll at least give our bodies a little protection."

"The holly I've got all over the house and hanging from my tree will take care of that." I pointed to the Christmas tree standing near the French door. Rebecca had helped me decorate the tree in what she called the Wicca style. On it, in addition to holly, we'd hung strings of dried rosebuds and cinnamon sticks. The ornaments were apples, oranges, and lemons—Rebecca told me this was how the Old Ones decorated their trees. A more modern tradition of brightly wrapped gifts filled the space beneath the tree. This should have been a joyful day. Children again, at least for a short while, we should have been on our knees, on the floor, torn paper strewn across the carpet.

"Dammit! I can't concentrate on football." Roger clicked off the television, and tossed the remote onto the table.

I took his hand. "I know you'd rather be with Harry."

He picked up my hand, and kissed it. "No. He was right. I belong here with you, making sure you're safe—you and Rebecca."

The cat poked her head out the kitchen door and glared at us.

"Yeah, Elvira. Making sure you stay safe, too."

My cat snorted, turned on her heels (or whatever it is a cat has), and returned to the kitchen. Having lived with this animal the last few years, I'd learned her reaction meant she objected to being an afterthought.

I smiled. "You mean, you need to make sure we're not getting into trouble."

"Nah. I've already figured out that can't be done." The smile Roger gave me in return for mine was only half of one.

He didn't have to tell me what so distracted him that even a football game failed to hold his attention. "I know," I said. "I also can't believe either Dan or Scott would be capable of murder."

Rebecca came from the kitchen carrying three white mugs. As she handed one to Roger and one to me, she said, "It has to be one of them, doesn't it? I mean, you said you told their wives. Their wives must have told them, and the next thing you know a bullet from one of their guns is in your front door." Sitting in the overstuffed wingback chair next to my bookcases, she sipped from her mug, then rested it on the lamp table. "So, if that's what happened, who else could it be?" She looked at us with the expression my high school geometry teacher used to use when, chalk all over his hands and shirt, he'd finished writing an equation on the blackboard, and declared, "QED."

Elvira strolled from the kitchen, and parked her hefty rear end at Rebecca's feet. Clearly, this nosy albino feline wanted to be part of our conversation. Looking up at Rebecca, she mewed, as if to say, *That sound's right to me.*

"I refuse to believe it," Roger said. "Geez, I've know those guys for years. Dan's so straight, when he was on patrol he wouldn't even take the free coffee Frankie's Donuts offered him—and that was damn good coffee."

Because I had also become friendly with Dan Cummings, I agreed with Roger's assessment. Still, as they say, I did so keeping my finger on the checker. After all, how well do you really know people you think of as friends? (Less than a year later, I would learn how very true that thought was.)

"What about Scott Potter," I said. "He told us he'd caught Derek Street at home after Street robbed Firth Jewelers. Maybe Kevin was Street's partner in the robbery—Scott told us he's sure Street had one, and Kevin had been his partner-in-crime in the past. Helping Street rob Firth's could be why Kevin came back to the Falls."

"Where are you goin' with this?" Roger sounded far from pleased with the direction in which my question might take us.

"Well, maybe when Scott Potter arrested Street, he didn't turn in all of the jewelry that had been stolen? If Kevin found out about that, he would've tried to blackmail Potter, and—"

"That makes sense to me," Rebecca broke in. "So Potter would've killed Kevin, and when he found out, Emlyn, that you knew of Kevin's connection to Street, he would've come after you to keep you from telling anyone."

Roger shook his head. "Emlyn, this theory sounds as convoluted as the plots in your stories."

"Can't help that, can I?" I shot back at him. "My recent books are about the cases *I* helped you solve."

Elvira snapped her head, and snorted. I took this to mean, *Darn right she did!*

Never one to let me get away with my usual sassiness—this was one of the strengths for which I loved the man—he opened his mouth to shoot back at me just as his cellphone rang. Holding up a finger that said this wasn't over yet, he left the sofa to retrieve his phone from the kitchen counter.

Standing at the entrance to the living room, he said, "Yeah, Chief. It's quiet here—well, quiet as it ever is when Emlyn wants to get into the middle of a case."

I stuck out my tongue at him.

Rebecca shook her head. "What a pair you two are. You totally belong together. Marry the man, already."

I glared at her.

When Elvira nodded, I glared at *her.*

Focused again on Roger, I heard him say, "I see. So, what did Dan tell you? He wasn't? Dammit!" His face creased into a deep frown.

"Dan wasn't what?" I said.

Again, Roger held up his forefinger. "Yeah, you're right, Chief. This isn't good. Do you know…? I see. You'll let me know what you find? Yeah, I'll be here."

When he clicked off his phone, this strong man looked as if he was ready to cry.

I struggled from the sofa, and hobbled to Roger's side. Reaching my arms around his waist, I looked up into his face. "What happened? What did Harry tell you?"

"You need to lie down again. I don't want you hurting yourself worse than you already are."

"Okay, I will." I said as he half carried me back to the sofa. "Now tell me what Harry said."

"He told me Scott Potter appears to be clear." Roger turned to Rebecca. "Looks like you were wrong about him being the perp. He was with Ginny at her parents' house from eight this morning till he got the call to go the precinct. Presuming the shots taken at you, Emlyn, are connected to Reinhart's murder, Scott can't be involved."

"And Dan?" I asked.

Roger took a deep breath, and rubbed his hand across his square jaw. "He never showed up. Lieutenant Juarez called every number the precinct had for him, even tried Alice's cellphone. She said when she woke up this morning, he wasn't in bed. What makes it worse for Dan, the bullet Crime Scene pulled from your doorframe? Ballistics told Harry it's from Dan's pistol."

My hand went to my mouth. "Dan tried to kill me? W-why? It doesn't make sense." Tears filled my eyes. "W-what possible motive could he have?"

"Don't know," Roger said. "None of this makes any sense. "Why shoot at you? Why kill Reinhart?"

Kevin Reinhart. Once I had loved that man enough to marry him. Though he'd hurt me, I'd grown stronger as a result, become independent. Sufficiently so, that in this holiday season a memory of our early years together brought an ounce of forgiveness for this man who had been killed. My eyes blurred by moisture, I looked at the Christmas tree. Gifts at its base, strings of dried rosebuds and cinnamon sticks wound around it, a white angel at its peak. An angel like the figurative tiny one that earlier had fluttered off when I reached for the solution to this puzzle. I looked down at the coffee table, at my ancient ancestor's *Book of Shadows*. Something in that book... The entry I'd read last night...

The imaginary angel appeared again in my living room, fluttering her wings just above Sarah Goode's book.

As if she also saw that tiny angel, Elvira leaped onto the coffee table, and pawed the old book.

I sniffed back my tears and wiped my eyes with the back of my hand. I brushed the cat aside. My lips tight, I grabbed the magnifying glass and the book. Carefully, I turned the brittle pages.

"What are you looking for?" Roger asked.

Rebecca clapped her hands. "She knows who did it—killed Kevin Reinhart and shot at her. You know, don't you Emlyn?"

My attention focused on the feint words, I ignored her. Twice I read, *Here do men, and it is rumored even a few women, lock their doors and drink while plotting what they might take that is not theirs.*

"Why did I assume it had to be…?" I mumbled.

"Had to be what?" Roger demanded.

I shook my head, and continued to read. *As in the Old Testament births, a twin child also was born…*

I closed the book and my eyes. My lips moving, I silently repeated those lines. As I did, that imaginary angel fluttered closer. "At the party, they sniped at each other." When I said that, the angel landed on my finger. I opened my eyes wide. "It has to be," I said. "Nothing else answers all the questions."

Roger sat up and slid to the edge of the sofa. "What questions, Emlyn? Dammit, talk to me!"

"Look at her eyes," Rebecca said. "She's figured it out."

I had. At least, I knew the *who*. I needed two more pieces of information to be certain of the *why*.

I sat back, holding Sarah Goode's book to my chest. "Roger, the computer database at the County Office Building—

does it have records of all the construction done in Niagara County?"

Elvira's head snapped from me to him. I swear the cat grinned.

"What does that have to do with—?" Rebecca said.

He raised his hand to stop her. The man's mind works quickly—that's another of the things I love about him. I could tell from the flicker of his eyes, my question had led him to same conclusion I'd reached. "Yeah," he said after just a few seconds. Reaching for his cell phone, he said, "Not the actual construction, but it has a record of all the licenses issued."

He punched numbers into his phone, then said, "Chief, forget Dan Cummings. Get hold of Alice. Yeah. I'll tell you why later."

I tapped his shoulder. "Tell Harry to have someone check the birth records—see if her mother had a second child."

He looked a question at me.

"Motive," I said. "Knowing that would wrap the package as nicely as those under my tree."

Into his phone, Roger repeated what I told him… Well, he left out the part about the packages under my tree. He listened for a second, then said, "What? Then get a team over here. You have to know where she's headed."

When he clicked off his phone, he said, "Emlyn, you and Rebecca, get upstairs. Now!"

"What?" Rebecca said.

"Why?" I said.

"Harry just left the Cummings's house. Alice wasn't there. Now move! Please."

Getting to a safe spot was good advice. But it came just a bit late.

Chapter Ten
Spoke Not a Word, But Went Straight to Work

I rose from the sofa and hobbled to the hall. Stopping there, I saw Roger arrange three of the sofa's throw pillows and the afghan, so someone looking through the mini-blinds on my French door would think a person was sitting on the sofa, watching television. That done, he pulled his off-duty pistol from the holster buckled to his left shin.

"Get upstairs," he hissed, and pushed me in that direction. Quickly, he flattened himself against the hall wall with his pistol at his chest, positioned to react if Alice's attack came from the front of my house or the back.

The phone on the kitchen counter rang. Though Roger shook his head, at the bottom of the stairs, I turned and answered it.

Urgency in Professor Nelson's voice, he said, "Emlyn, I was adjusting the lights on my tree, and saw someone run past the back of my house, headed in your direction."

"The back yard!" I shouted.

His pistol still positioned against his chest, Roger rushed toward the French door and knelt behind the Christ-mas tree.

Watching this, I stood with the phone at my ear.

"I've called 9-1-1," Professor Nelson said. "They should be—"

His voice got lost in a cacophony of sound and sight. The *wroo wroo* of sirens raced down River Road. Three cracks. Gunshots. A pane of the French door shattered, glass scattered. The pillows placed like a person on my sofa exploded. Fibers of cotton and wads of foam flew up, left and right.

I dove to the floor.

Four more cracks. The sound of glass breaking. A cry of pain echoed around me.

My eyes closed, I prayed, *Not Roger! Please, God. "Goddess of the moon, protector of the earth, stand before my man. Don't let it be him that got hit.*

Running in my yard, voices shouting.

"Over there, near the bushes."

"Watch it. She's trying to get up."

"Look out for the gun!"

Another shot rang.

"Drop your weapon! Lie on the ground!"

I heard the French door swing open. Roger shouted, "Cuff her!"

I got to my knees. He was okay. "Thank you, God. Thank you Goddess."

"Collins, call a bus," Roger said. "Scott, phone the chief.

Elvira's head poked out from the skirt around my overstuffed chair. She looked around.

Rebecca pounded down the stairs. "Emlyn." She knelt beside me. "Are you okay?"

Much like my cat, I glanced around. "My house... The sofa... The French door..." Unlike my cat, I started to cry.

My friend tossed her long salt and pepper braid over her shoulder. Leaning back on her heels, she examined my legs, arms, and torso.

"I'm all right, but my house..." I wiped away my tears with the back of my hand.

"Is that blood on your face?" Rebecca licked her finger, and rubbed my cheek. "You're not cut there." She looked down. I followed her eyes, and saw a few red drops on the polished wood. "Let me see your hand," she said.

Roger came through the French door, and ran to us. "Are you okay?" he said to me. He looked at Rebecca. "Is she okay?"

She showed him my hand. "It looks like a splinter from the doorframe cut her. Doesn't look bad."

He wrapped me in his arms. "I told you to get upstairs. Didn't I tell you that?" Finished scolding, he hugged and kissed me.

Rebecca got to her feet. "I've got something in my bag that'll take care of her wound." She went to the kitchen—hanging up the receiver of my house phone on her way—and returned with a vial.

Is there anything she doesn't carry in her bag, I wondered.

While she applied some kind of oil, then wrapped my finger in gauze, I looked through the open French door. Three officers were on their knees, surrounding a figure in a black hooded coat lying on the ground. "Is she…?"

"Uh-uh," Roger said. "I just got her in the shoulder." He lifted me, and carried me to the sofa. Putting me down, he eyed the damage the bullets had done. "Gonna need a couple of new pillows."

More sirens came down River Road. In what seemed to be no more than a minute, EMTs carrying a folding gurney joined the officers in my yard. Harry came through my front door, followed by my next door neighbor.

"Everyone all right in here?" Harry asked as he took Rebecca's arm.

Professor Nelson looked over his shoulder. "You okay, Emlyn? I heard shots and then the phone dropped."

"Thanks for the heads-up, Prof," Roger said. "It saved our asses."

"Anything I can do?"

"No. Thanks," Harry said. "We've got everything under control."

When Professor Nelson went out my front door, Scott Potter came in through the French door. "I read Alice her rights while they wheeled her out of the yard. She lawyered up."

"Figures," Roger said. He came to the sofa, and knelt beside me. "Maybe it's time I read you *your* rights."

"Me? What did I do, officer?"

He gave me his most knee-weakening smile. "You have the right to marry me—"

I smacked his arm.

Chapter Eleven
Giving A Nod, Up the Chimney He Rose

The evening of Christmas Day, every seat in my living room was filled. Rebecca sat in the overstuffed wingback chair. Harry had pulled a dining room chair next to her. Scott Potter and Ginny sat side-by-side, holding hands on the sofa. Roger and I were in the straight-back dining room chairs my guy insisted would be better for my sore lower back. Elvira had curled up under the coffee table. When Harry, Roger, and Scott had returned from interrogating Alice Cummings, they brought enough food from Como's Restaurant to feed an army—or, at least a squad of hungry cops. Now the dinner plates were piled on the kitchen counter. The doors of my étagère in which I kept my liquor were open, and wine glasses were in everybody's hands.

"Has someone gotten hold of Dan?" Ginny asked.

"I spoke to him," Harry said. "He called in. He'd driven down to Erie early this morning. Alice woke him, told him his mother had just called, because his father had a stroke."

"Convenient way to get him outta town and get hold of his service pistol while he was away," Roger said. "I pre-sume the stroke was a lie."

"Got that right." Harry's lips were tight as he shook his head.

Scott sipped his wine. "Set him up to take the fall for killing Reinhart."

Ginny pulled her husband's arm to her chest. "God, Dan must be so devastated."

"I don't know." Harry rubbed his cheek. "He must've had a clue she was up to something."

Scott put down his wine glass. "But, something like this?"

Harry shrugged.

I thought about the way Dan and Alice had sniped at each other in the bar last night. My first instinct had been correct. Theirs wasn't a happy marriage. *Was that because of the difference in their ages,* I wondered. *Did a twelve-year difference become more extreme as they got older?* I glanced at Roger who was almost eight years older than me. I loved the man, and I was sure Alice had loved Dan when she agreed to marry him fifteen years ago.

My mental meandering was interrupted when Scott said, "How'd you figure it was Alice that did Reinhart, Emlyn?"

"Yeah, how'd you get there this time?" Roger wrapped his arm around my shoulders, and grinned. "I was with you the whole time, so you can't claim magic gave you the answer."

"Magic?" Ginny said.

Elvira lifted her head from her paws, and looked at me with an expression I took to mean, *Uh-oh.*

My cheeks felt so hot, I'm sure I was blushing from my neck all the way up to my red hair. In the two years since I'd learned of my heritage, I'd taken great care to be sure no one knew Sarah Goode's craft ran in my genes. My God, if Grace Linden found out about that, she'd tell all of Niagara Falls. "Emlyn Goode thinks she's a real witch," people would say. I'd become a laughing stock. Kids would toilet paper my house even when it wasn't Halloween. I'd be forced to move, maybe to Africa…

Rebecca saved me from the need of an immediate departure to the *Dark Continent*, when she laughed, and said, "The way Emlyn's mind works really *is* magic."

Roger pecked a kiss on my cheek and poured us both more wine.

"So, how did ya come up with it?" Scott asked.

I took a deep breath. "I'm a writer. Part of my job is to notice things."

"Like what?" Ginny asked.

"Well, like Alice, Dan, and you, Scott, each dis-appearing into the stairwell for a while before we went into the ballroom for dinner. I'd noticed Kevin slinking around before that, but caught no sight of him afterwards. So, he had to have been killed when we were in the bar."

"Why do you say that?" Rebecca asked. "He could've been killed anytime while we ate."

"No, he couldn't. It had to be before then, or the killer wouldn't have been able to put Kevin's tongue in Roger's Secret Santa gift box. I had been watching that exit to the stairwell all the time we were in the bar. You three were the only ones who went there. So, it had to be one of you."

"Whew." Scott laughed, and wiped his brow. "We'd all better be careful about what we do when you're around."

"You don't know the half of it." Roger's grin was so bright it might have lit a city.

Harry leaned from his chair. "Yeah, I get that, but why Alice?"

I had to be careful here not to let on that the answer came from what I'd read in old Sarah's book. "That, um…" I chewed on my lower lip. "Well, it was a guess. I knew Kevin would only come back here if there was a quick dollar to be made. When you told us, Scott, you were sure Derek Street had a partner in the jewel story robbery, I remembered he and Kevin had been partners before, so I would've bet anything he was the partner in the heist."

Scott looked from Harry, to Roger, to me. "I still don't see how you got from them to Alice, Emlyn."

I sighed. "That was another guess. "I wondered how Street would've known just the right night to pull the robbery. Knowing Alice operated a computer at the county office, I realized she would've known the days on which construction was being done at Firth's. After that… Well the rest fell into place. And, before you ask, I guessed she had to be related in some way to Street—who else but a relative would she have called on to break into the jewelry story."

"Good guess," Harry said. "It only took our depart-ment's IT guy ten minutes to find out Street was Alice's half-brother."

When I glanced at Scott, his brow was wrinkled. "Alice Cummings discovered the body—her and that waitress did. That's something that threw me off. Why would a killer find her victim?"

Roger scratched his chin. "While I was interviewing them, Alice said she saw the waitress go into the stairwell to smoke, and followed her. A few minutes later, the waitress told me it was Alice that suggested they smoke in the stairwell. I didn't catch that at the time—probably because Alice was a friend.

"She did that to throw everyone off her scent," I said. As you asked, Scott, why would the killer be the one that found the victim?

Now Rebecca tilted her head and her eyes narrowed. "But if Kevin was involved in the robbery, why did she kill him?"

"How can you ask me that? You knew my ex."

She laughed. "The God and Goddess help me, I did. With Street in jail, he would've gone to her for his cut, and the Christmas party was probably the only place he could catch up with her without being seen."

"Exactly. And now Alice had a problem. Scott, I'm guessing the jewelry you found in Street's apartment was about half of what the guys stole."

He nodded. "About that. Yeah."

"I think Alice needed the rest of it to escape from her marriage to Dan and set up a new life. While we were in the bar, she talked about going to that IT convention in Miami. Remember, Ginny? So I'm also guessing she planned a second leg to her trip—to some country with no extradition back to the U.S."

Roger smiled at me, and picked up my thought. "So when Kevin came to her for his cut, she would've refused to give it to him. She did that, your sleaze-ball ex would've threatened to turn her in."

Rebecca held out her glass. "I still don't see why she cut off Kevin's tongue and put it in Roger's gift?"

"I'd bet it didn't matter whose gift she put it in," Harry said, as he rose to fetch a fresh wine bottle from the étagère. "She did that to send a message to Street—he'd better not rat her out or the same thing would happen to him."

Rebecca's eyes went wide. "In jail?"

"You'd ever met the guy, you'd understand," Scott said. "He sure as hell ain't the brightest bulb."

"Amen to that." Harry raised his glass. "Here's to all those crooked dim bulbs."

"You got that right, Chief," Roger said. "They were any brighter, we might never catch 'em."

Laughing, we sipped our wine.

My cat's head came up, and she glared at us. Her *meeeow*, seemed to say, *Pipe down, would you please. I'm trying sleep.*

"Knock it off, Elvira," Rebecca said. "This is a party."

"Thank you," I told her. "Now, I have another toast—one more fitting to this season." I raised my glass to Roger. "Here's to loved ones…" I tilted it toward Rebecca and Harry. "…to old friends…" Now, I tilted my glass to Ginny and Scott on the sofa. "…and new friends." Finally, I turned and raised my glass to the boarded up French door. "To all the friends we've yet to meet. Happy Christmas to all!"

Elvira slithered from under the table, stood, and sauntered down the hall. At the steps, she turned to look at us. With a snort that could only mean, *To all good night!* She scampered upstairs to my bedroom.

Susan Lynn Solomon

Formerly a Manhattan entertainment attorney and a contributing editor to the quarterly art magazine SunStorm Fine Art, Susan Lynn Solomon now lives in Niagara Falls, New York, the setting of many of her stories.

Since 2007 her short stories have appeared in a number of literary journals. These stories include, Abigail Bender (awarded an Honorable Mention in a short romance competition), Ginger Man, Elvira, The Memory Tree, Going Home, Reunion, Yesterday's Wings, Smoker's Lament, Kaddish, and Sabbath (nominated for the 2013 Best of the Net). A collection of her short stories, Voices In My Head, has been released by Solstice Publishing.

Susan Solomon is also the author of the Emlyn Goode Mysteries. A finalist in M&M's Chanticleer's Mystery & Mayhem Novel Contest, and a finalist for the 2016 Book Excellence Award, her first Emlyn Goode Mystery novel, The Magic of Murder, has received rave reviews, as has the novelette, Bella Vita, and the novel, Dead Again, which is a finalist for the 2017

McGrath House Indie Book of the Year Award. In the latest Emlyn Goode Mystery novelette, The Day the Music Died, Ms. Solomon once again demonstrates that murder can have sense of humor.

Social Media Links

Facebook:
http://www.facebook.com/susanlynnsolomon

LinkedIn:
https://www.linkedin.com/in/susan-solomon-8183b129

Website: http://www.susanlynnsolomon.com

Twitter:
https://twitter.com/susanlynnsolom1
@susanlynnsolom1

If you enjoyed this story, check out these other Solstice Publishing books by Susan Lynn Solomon:

The Magic of Murder

When his partner is discovered in a frozen alley with eight bullets in his chest, Niagara Falls Police Detective Roger Frey swears vengeance. But Detective Chief Woodward has forbidden him or anyone else on the detective squad to work the case. Emlyn Goode knows Roger will disobey his boss, which will cost him his job and his freedom. Because she cares for him more than she'll admit, she needs to stop him. Desperate, she can think of but one way.

Emlyn recently learned she's a direct descendant of a woman hanged as a witch in 1692. She has a book filled with arcane recipes and chants passed down through her family. Possessed of, or perhaps by a vivid imagination, she intends to use these to solve Jimmy's murder before Roger takes revenge on the killer. But she's new to this "witch thing," and needs help from her friend Rebecca Nurse, whose ancestor also took a short drop from a Salem tree. Rebecca's not much better at deciphering the ancient directions, and while the women stumble over spell after spell, the number possible killers grows. When Chief Woodward's wife is shot and a bottle bomb bursts through Emlyn's window, it becomes clear she's next on the killer's list.

https://bookgoodies.com/a/B015OQO5LO

Dead Again

When Emlyn Goode's mother returns to Niagara Falls for a high school reunion, so does murder. During the reunion, a woman's body is found in the ladies room. Is this killing connected to one that occurred 40 years before in the woods below the town of Lewiston? Harry Woodward, a young police officer working his first murder case suspected Emlyn's mother of the crime, although there wasn't enough evidence to arrest her.

Home from a year-long leave, Harry—now the Niagara Falls Chief of Detectives—together with Emlyn's friend, Detective Roger Frey, investigates the latest killing. Distraught over indications her mother might have been involved in both murders, Emlyn, with her cohort, Rebecca Nurse, sets out to prove otherwise. But, danger lurks in the shadows when amateurs—even ones with witchy skills—get involved with murder.

http://bookgoodies.com/a/B01N0OA1IV

Bella Vita

A car burns in the parking lot behind Bella Vita Hair Salon. The corpse in the front seat has a short sword pushed into his ribs. Beneath the car is a cast-iron cauldron filled with flowers. This seems to be a sacrificial rite Rebecca Nurse had been teaching Emlyn Goode. But is it? The corpse has been identified as George Malone, and earlier on this summer solstice day, he and his wife had severe argument. Could it be that Angela Malone has murdered her husband? Prodded by Elvira, an overly-large albino cat that wants the case solved so she can get some sleep, to Rebecca's dismay Emlyn again dips into her ancient relatives Book of Shadows to find the answer before her friend and neighbor, Detective Roger Fry, can.

http://bookgoodies.com/a/B01I01WEWW

The Day the Music Died

A rock star's murder leaves Emlyn Goode questioning everything she knows about herself.

Amanda Stone, a rock and roll icon who vanished at the peak of her career in 1986, has returned to her hometown of Niagara Falls. She brings with her a message that causes Emlyn Goode to question everything she knows about herself. When Stone is murdered, Emlyn must use the craft her ancient relative wrote of in a Book of Shadows to solve the crime. If she fails, she'll never know if what Stone told her is true.

https://bookgoodies.com/a/B0747V1DPT

Voices In My Head

In The Magic of Murder, Susan Lynn Solomon let readers laugh at the antics of an albino cat and a witch. Now, in nine short tales she takes a serious look at relationships and their impact on characters who confront their pasts.

A young soldier returns, changed by his war. A young British girl faces the people of her town after parental abuse. An older man who as a teenager fled his hometown, returns when his childhood girlfriend begs a favor. A radical of the '70s leaves the cemetery after her mother's funeral, searching for where her life will lead.

In these stories and five others, Solomon explores the persistence of memory and the promise of hope.

http://bookgoodies.com/a/B01FURPIZE